CYRIL
The Seagull

CYRIL
The Seagull

Patricia Lines

Illustrated by Kim LaFave

NIGHTWOOD EDITIONS

Cyril the seagull lived with his family in a small bay where the water seldom showed more than a ripple. Until he was six months old, his mother didn't allow him to go out of the bay.

But when he was big enough to
explore the straits, Cyril soon learned
to follow Joe's ferry boat. Each day it
came along at the same time and Joe
always threw delicious scraps overboard
for the gulls to eat.

Joe wore a white apron and a large white
hat. When he threw the scraps for Cyril and
his family he made seagull noises and laughed
a happy laugh. Joe was so jolly and friendly
Cyril loved to be near him.

Cyril liked nothing better than to perch on the rail of the big ferry and chatter to Joe about catching minnows and crabs along the shore. Even though Joe didn't know what Cyril was saying, he made friendly cooing noises that showed he had a special place in his heart for the noisy young gull.

Cyril enjoyed every minute of his first warm, glorious summer. It wasn't until the fall, when the winds blew cold and the waves began their wild dance, that Cyril's happiness turned to gloom. One windy fall day as he rode a big dark wave, his tummy give a sickly heave. He felt dizzy and whimpered to his mother to lead him ashore.

"You've been eating too much junk food from that darned ferry boat," his mother scolded. Cyril shook his head. He'd had a tummy ache before from swallowing a starfish too fast, but this felt much worse. He had never felt so terrible in his life. Cyril knew the worst thing that can happen to any seagull had happened to him. He was seasick!

Telling the rest of his family was the hardest part. His big brother Jerry teased him cruelly.

"Cyril, the seasick seagull! Who every heard of a seasick seagull? My baby brother's afraid of the water!"

All his brothers and sisters and cousins laughed—all except pretty Betty Featherlight, who stood up for Cyril.

"Cyril can't help it," she would cry. "Don't be mean!"

But it was true. Cyril was afraid. He was
afraid the sickly, sinking feeling in the pit of
his tummy and the dizzy feeling in his head
would come back if he went out on the
tumbling waves again. For his mother's sake
and Betty's sake Cyril wanted to swim back
out into the tossing seas with big brother
Jerry and all the other gulls, but when he
remembered those awful seasick feelings, he
just couldn't force his pink little toes into the
water.

He crawled away to a protected place on a mossy ledge. There he huddled day after day, feeling sad and hungry as he watched the other gulls frolic and fish for their dinner in the surging swells. On days when the fog was thick, he would listen to the moan of the fog horn in the lighthouse on the rocky point. Before the fog horn was put there, many ships like Joe's crashed into the rocks and sank. Now the moan of the horn warned Joe and others to stay away when the fog blocked their vision.

One winter day the wind blew harder than ever before. The storm was so frightening Cyril's whole family crowded into his hideout on the mossy ledge. He was happy to have his mother and Betty with him, but he was scared, too. Big trees crashed down in the wind, and giant waves pounded the shore. Then fog came down like a grey curtain across the bay.

It was a long time since Cyril had eaten and he felt hungry. He wished he was out at sea again gobbling up scraps behind Joe's ferry boat. His tummy told him it was time for Joe's ferry boat to be coming. He hoped Joe would be careful in the fog.

Suddenly, Cyril realized he could not hear the moan of the fog horn. He listened hard, but all he could hear was the howl of the wind. Then he heard something else. It was the far-away rumble of Joe's ferry boat coming through the fog towards the point.

Without the horn to warn it away, Joe's ferry would surely crash into the rocks!

Without stopping to think of his own fear, he decided he must do something to help his friend.

"Cyril, where are you going?" his mother cried. "You can't go out in this weather!"

Betty looked worried.

"I'm going to the lighthouse on the point," Cyril told them. "The fog horn has stopped moaning and Joe's ferry boat will crash into the rocks and sink. I have to help!"

Before they could say any more Cyril flew off into the storm.

The wind was so strong it tossed Cyril onto his back and blew him in the wrong direction. He couldn't fly, so he had to swim. He splashed down upon the tossing seas and paddled furiously with his little pink feet. The waves heaved him up and slapped him down, but he kept on paddling and paddling.

Finally he saw the rocky point. The fog horn was still silent and the lighthouse was still dark. What could be wrong? Through the scream of the wind he heard the rumble of the ferry boat's engines growing louder. It was only minutes from hitting the rocky point!

In a panic, Cyril scrambled up the rocks to the lighthouse. The cause of the trouble was clear. The waves had thrown a chunk of driftwood up against the lighthouse and it had become stuck in the fog horn. With all the strength he had left, Cyril put his back against the lighthouse and pushed on the driftwood as hard as he could with his tired pink feet. The chunk moved a little, but not enough. Cyril tried again, harder this time. All of a sudden the wood broke loose and a deafening moan burst from the fog horn. He'd done it!

Just in time,
Joe's ferry boat heard
the moan of the horn and
swerved away from the rocks.
Clinging to a juniper bush to keep
from being blown out to sea, Cyril
was sure he saw a familiar figure wave
a big white hat from the back of the ferry
as it passed safely into the bay.

For a long time Cyril clung to the juniper bush. After many hours more the wind died down and the fog cleared away so he could once again see across the bay. Where he had struggled through the huge waves the sea was now glassy calm.

He was too stiff and sore to move, but he saw something moving towards him. A flock of white seagulls was fanning out across the blue sky. In a minute his mother and brothers and sisters and cousin were all around him, all squawking at once.

"Cyril! Are you alright?" called his Mother.

"You saved Joe's ferry boat," cried Betty. "You're a hero, Cyril!"

"I thought you were afraid of waves," grinned big brother Jerry, just a little bit jealous.

It was only then that Cyril realized he had struggled through the biggest waves of the year and hadn't thought of being seasick once. He wanted to help his friend Joe so much, he hadn't had time to think of his own trouble. Now he knew he would never be afraid of the sea again, no matter how big the waves.

"Oh, look," someone cried. "The ferry boat is coming back, and Joe is throwing out scraps!"

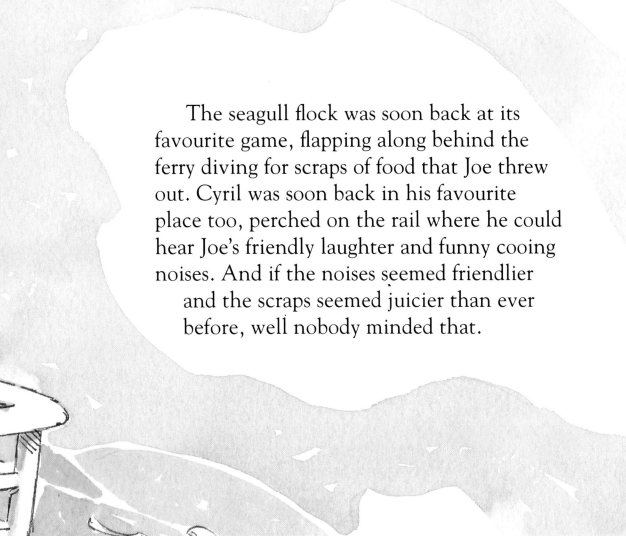

The seagull flock was soon back at its favourite game, flapping along behind the ferry diving for scraps of food that Joe threw out. Cyril was soon back in his favourite place too, perched on the rail where he could hear Joe's friendly laughter and funny cooing noises. And if the noises seemed friendlier and the scraps seemed juicier than ever before, well nobody minded that.

NIGHTWOOD EDITIONS
P.O. Box 411
Madeira Park, BC Canada V0N 2H0

Design by Roger Handling

Canadian Cataloguing in Publication Data

Lines, Patricia.
    Cyril the seasick seagull

    "A Nightwood book."
    ISBN 0-88971-048-1

    I. LaFave, Kim.   II. Title.
    PS8573.I53C9 1991   jC813'.54   C91-091418-4
    PZ7.L56Cy 1991